To Dylan,
Happy Na, Na, Na, Na
Daddy Rabbit
2003

MAЯTY

(Sometimes written as "Marty" on Earth)

THE LITTLE LOST MARTIAN

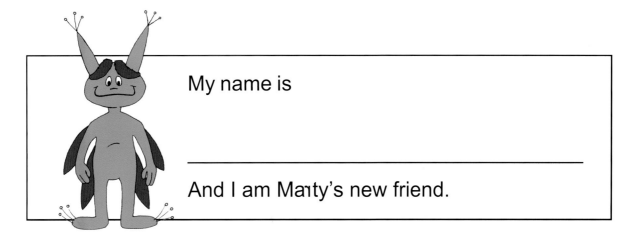

My name is

_____

And I am Maтty's new friend.

Besides Daddy Rabbit, the only person known to have ever seen Maтty is a girl named Kimberly. She peeked during Santa's and Maтty's visit to her house on Christmas Eve.

Thank you, Kimberly, for the picture you drew of Maтty, showing us what this lovable little Martian looks like.

Thank you, Kevin, for taking Kimberly's drawing and doing the wonderful illustrations in this book.

Daddy Rabbit, obviously you're on the inside track with Santa and Maтty. Thank you for sharing this story with us. Hope we've done a good job of passing it on to all the children of the world.

Dear Parent,

This is the first in our "Book of Essence" collection. The goal is to bring fun, adventure, and a meaningful message to your child. We hope you enjoy it too. We welcome your comments and inquiries.
Sincerely,

Willum Fowler

Published by The Fowler Companies, Inc.
1417 Alford Ave.
Birmingham, Alabama 35226

Printed in Hong Kong

Publisher's Cataloging-in-Publication
(Provided by Quality Books, Inc.)

Daddy Rabbit.
    Marty the little lost Martian / as told by Daddy Rabbit ;
illustrated by Kevin Johnson. – 1ˢᵗ ed.
    p. cm.
    Preassigned LCCN: 97-94728
    ISBN: 0-9661365-0-0
    Summary: Santa's toy production is running behind, but a
little lost Martian arrives just in time to help.

    1. Santa Claus-Juvenile fiction. 2. Christmas-Juvenile
fiction. 3. Martians-Juvenile fiction.   I. Title.

PZ7.D1275Ma 1998   **[E]**
                                            QB197-41606

10   9   8   7   6   5   4   3   2   1

"Book of Essence"   Number 1

MARTY

THE LITTLE LOST MARTIAN

As told by Daddy Rabbit

Illustrated by Kevin Johnson

One fine Martian day, Marty decided to take a short vacation to Phobos, one of Mars' moons. Now Phobos is very cold and always has lots of snow. This was right up Marty's alley because he just loved to snow-bathe. Martians love snow, you know. "I can hardly wait to start soaking up that snow," thought Marty. "When I get back, instead of being pale pea green like I am now, I'll have a deep dark-green snow tan."

So Marty boarded his flying saucer called the "Apple Pie," and off they went into the red Martian sky.

Now the Apple Pie wasn't just your old ordinary everyday kind of flying saucer. It had a very smart computer brain that could not only pilot itself, but could also speak in a Martian language called Na-Na. You might say that the Apple Pie had a mind of its own.

The Apple Pie was very good company for Marty on trips. To pass the time they would entertain themselves with a game called X-Toe. X-Toe is kind of like Tic-Tac-Toe. They would play it on the Apple Pie's monitor screen.

Marty's problems all began while playing a game of X-Toe. He and the Apple Pie had become so involved, they unknowingly flew right past Phobos.

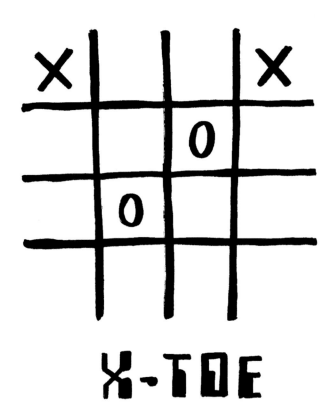

X-TOE

When they realized what had happened, it was too late. Marty and the Apple Pie were desperately lost deep in space. Home was far away.

Marty and the Apple Pie traveled many days in search of Mars, but the more they looked, the more lost they got among the stars. Finally Marty just gave up and cried himself to sleep. All he could dream about was home.

Then all of a sudden Marty was awakened by the Apple Pie's voice. "Na-Na-Na-Naaa, Na-Na-Naa, Na-Na-Na," it shouted, almost blowing a circuit.

"What is it!" cried Marty as he raced toward the window to see what the fuss was all about.

There it was, a beautiful glistening planet, all blue and green with swirling marble clouds. "And look! Snow white polar caps! That must be Earth ahead!" Marty shouted, his voice trembling with excitement.

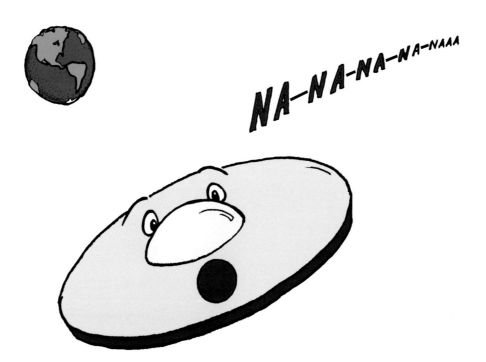

Marty had heard about Earth back home, but no one had ever landed there or made contact with Earthlings. Martians are very shy you know. But Marty was so tired and weary he said, "Fiddlesticks, I think I'll go where the cold winds blow and rest my little green head."

Meanwhile on Earth, it just so happened that it was Christmas Eve and Santa and his helpers were having problems of their own. They were running far behind, and there was no way to get all the toys made in time.

"What are we to do?" cried Mrs. Santa. "There will be so many disappointed boys and girls if we don't get the toys finished."

Santa started scratching his head, stroking his snow white beard, and taking giant puffs on his pipe. "Dear," he said, "we must have a miracle. It's just as simple as that."

No sooner had Santa gotten the words out than there appeared a light in the North Pole Sky. It was Marty's flying saucer, the Apple Pie. Closer and closer came the brilliant glow till it was brighter than daytime on the new fallen snow. Whirring Na-Na-Na-Naas were all you could hear as the saucer gently landed in front of Santa, his helpers, Mrs. Santa, and all the reindeer.

Then out stepped Marty.

"I am Santa Claus, and who might you be, my little green friend?"

"I'm Marty, a little lost Martian." Marty shyly exclaimed.

"You look very tired," said Santa. "Come in, and let's talk over a nice cup of hot chocolate."

"Hot chocolate?" said Marty.

Well Marty told Santa of his misadventure and how the Apple Pie had gone astray. Santa paused a moment, and then with a twinkle in his eye and a great big "Ho, Ho, Ho" he said, "Marty, I can help you find your way back home all right. Mars is one of the planets I'll use to guide my sleigh tonight." But then Santa's eyes saddened as he told Marty about his dilemma.

Marty thought for a moment, and then all of a sudden his antennas lit up and he said, "Santa, I think I can help solve your problem right away."

Marty didn't know it then, but he would save Christmas Day.

Now Marty had wondrous things they say, like a little red gun with a toy-making ray. Zip, Zap and out of thin air, thousands of toys appeared everywhere. There were dolls and drums and teddy bears, bikes and trikes and trains to spare. Marty finished the toys in the flash of a light, as Santa and his helpers chuckled with delight.

Then Marty said in a puzzling voice, "I'm sure glad I could help you this way, but tell me Santa, what is Christmas Day?"

"Why Christmas is, ah ...," Santa stuttered in amazement, then stopped, rubbed his belly, and let out a big "Ho, Ho, Ho. Now Marty," said Santa, "come with me. I want to give you a gift of great rarity."

So they loaded Santa's sleigh and the Apple Pie, and off they went into the twinkling sky.

As they flew high above Earth, Santa pointed to the heavens. There it was, bright and red among a million stars, Marty's home, the planet Mars.

Home ... it seemed far away, but being with Santa was so wonderfully exciting that Marty became less homesick with every minute that ticked away.

They stopped at every house, and down the chimneys they went, quiet as a church mouse and quick as a wink. They filled all the stockings from Santa's toy sack and found lots of goodies left out for them to snack. There were cookies and cakes with icing on top.

Marty munched and munched till he was about to pop. "No wonder you're so round and jolly, Santa," said Marty.

Santa just let out a big "Ho, Ho, Ho, *burp,* excuse me!"

There were special notes from the children, sometimes Mom and Dad too, wishing Santa a Merry Christmas, signing off with "We Love You."

Now Marty saw things he had never seen. Santa let him look into all the children's dreams. In those visions were laughing eyes and hearts full of Joy. Christmas Love was shared by every girl and boy.

So this was Santa's gift, the greatest heard of, Marty received **Christmas Joy** and **Love**.

After the night's work was done and they were on their way back to the North Pole, Marty just couldn't get out of his mind how great it was being with Santa and receiving the gift of Christmas Joy and Love.

When they arrived they found to their surprise that Mrs. Santa and the helpers had prepared a big party for Marty, the guest of honor. What a great time they all had!

After the grand celebration was over, things got very quiet. "Well, Marty," said Santa, "I suppose you will be wanting to head back home to Mars now."

Then things got so very quiet that you could have heard a pin drop on the new fallen snow. Marty just stood there and looked straight ahead as a big tear rolled down his cheek.

After a minute or so Marty cried out, "Santa I want to stay. I'll be your little green helper forever from this day."

Then a great big cheer came from Santa, his helpers, Mrs. Santa, and all the reindeer. They began to laugh and sing as the Apple Pie led in perfect pitch and rhythm with Na-Na-Na-Na-Na-Naa, Na-Na-Na-Naa!

So this is the story of Marty the little lost Martian. Now if you should be awakened on Christmas Eve by jingling bells and strange whirring sounds, don't be frightened. It will just be Santa, his reindeer, Marty, and the Apple Pie. But only listen, don't open your eyes.

Well, maybe one little peek.

THE END

MARTY

(Sometimes written as "Marty" on Earth)

THE LITTLE LOST MARTIAN

Marty the little lost Martian, his saucer had gone astray,
Marty didn't even know it then, but he would save christmas day. And he said

"Na - Na Na- Naa, Na - Na - Na - Na - Na - Na - Naa, It looks like Earth a - head, I

think I'll go where the cold winds blow, and rest my little green head." Now

Santa was running way behind, he couldn't get the toys all made in time, Then a

Light appeared in the North Pole sky, It was Marty's flying saucer called "The Apple Pie." Now

Marty had wondrous things they say, like a little red gun with a toy-making ray, he

Finished the toys in a flash of light, as Santa and his helpers chuckled with delight.

Marty the little lost Martian, his saucer had gone astray,
Marty didn't even know it then, but he had saved Christmas Day.

And he said "Na-na-na-naa, Na-na-na-na-na-na-na, I'm glad I could help this way, but
Na-na-na-naa, Na-na-na-na-na-na-naa, tell me, What is Christmas Day?"

Now, Santa said "Marty come and go with me, I want to give you a gift of great rarity;"
So they loaded Santa's sleigh and the Apple Pie, and off they went into the twinkling sky.

Marty saw things he had never seen, like laughing eyes in all the children's dream's,
Santa's gift was the greatest heard of, Marty received CHRISTMAS JOY AND LOVE.

Marty the little lost Martian, his saucer had gone astray,
Marty didnt even know it, but he'd get the greatest gift of Christmas Day.

And he said, Na-na-na-naa, Na-na-na-na-na-na-naa,
Santa I want to stay, I'll be your little green helper, forever from this day.

And they sang Na-na-na-naa, Na-na-na-na-na-na-na,
Na-na-na-naa-na-na-naa......